# Quentin the Squirrel

introducing

& his collection
of silly poems

**David**: Thank you to Mona, Rita and David
for telling me the secret of life: "Fear tells lies"


**Sue**: For Ezra James Edwards

First published 2020 by MEBooks

46 Poppy Drive, Ampthill, Bedfordshire, MK45 2AW

This edition published 2020


The right of David Anderson to be identified as author and Sue Dooley to be identified as illustrator of this
work has been asserted by them in accordance with the Copyright, Designs and Patents Act 1988


This book has been typeset in Brandon Grotesque


Printed in the United Kingdom • ISBN number 978-1-8381933-0-0

A catalogue record for this book is available from the British Library

**www.pepthepoet.co.uk**

# Quentin the Squirrel

introducing & his collection of silly poems

words by **David Anderson**

illustrated by **Sue Dooley**

additional artwork by **Matthew Edwards**

# Contents

# Quentin the Squirrel

*(To be recited in a Yorkshire accent)*

Quentin the Squirrel
was agile and quick.
Incredibly nimble
and totally slick.

He could climb.
He could run.
He could jump.
He could fly.

A talented all-rounder.
A wonderful guy.

To relax he would swim
with the ease of a fish.
His fur he would preen.
His tail he would swish.

He'd swim on his back
and when we asked why?
He'd reply with a smile,
"Oh, it keeps me nuts dry!"

## Norma the Newt
*(To be recited in a Liverpudlian accent)*

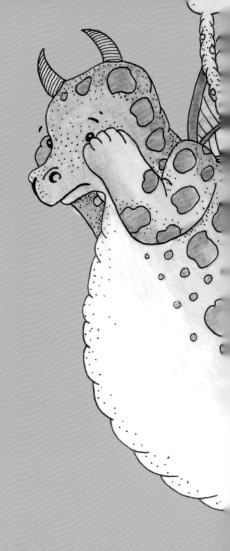

I'm Norma the Newt.
I'm not very cute
but I'm okay with that.

I live over the road
from Terry the Toad.
Well, the pond, to be exact.

I'm not fibbin', but being an amphibian
has its problems too.
See, our Terry's a red
an' I'm 100% blue.

Well, Terry's me fella
an' I love him t' pieces.
He worries about me
cos I'm an endangered species.

I said, "Listen, mate,
I'll be here forever.
So, stand by your bed
an' just look clever."

8

## James My Fiery Bum Dragon
*(To be recited in a Black Country accent)*

My name is Ellis an' I don't like braggin'.
For my sixth birthday, I got a pet dragon.

He is ever so cool. His name is James.
When he trumps, he throws out flames.

Fiery farts are becoming a problem,
especially for James and his fiery bottom.

He let one rip whilst in the kitchen.
Now my cat looks like a barbecued chicken.

At school, he gets such funny looks.
His bottom burped and burnt my books.

He can't eat beans or Brussels sprouts.
Just in case he lets one out.

My sister Maysie is looking glum.
No one likes a dragon
with a flame-throwing bum.

# What Did You Learn in School Today?

What did you learn in school today?
A mother asked her son.
What did I learn in school today?
Hang on, I'll tell you, Mum.

I learned we have metatarsals in our toes.
I learned in Peru, they wear different clothes.
I learned that Sir's got big hairs up his nose.

I learned that a nonagon has nine straight sides.
I learned that a fly has five large eyes.
I learned today that fear tells lies.

I learned that you can't cheat in a test.
I learned that the sun rests in the West.
I learned that Miss has coffee breath.

I learned King Arthur lived in Camelot.
I learned the desert is very, very hot.
I learned that the dinner lady trumps a lot.

I learned that Aztecs are long since forgotten.
I learned that sprouts are vile and rotten.
I leaned that Mrs Minihane has a big wobbly
...chair.

So, Mum, I hope that's okay.
That's all I learned in school today.

## Tony the Butterfly
*(To be recited in a Lancashire accent)*

Hello, I'm Tony.

Mi life so far has bin a proper thriller.
See, I were born a caterpillar.
Well, actually an egg, to be precise.
Laid by mi mum, that were nice.

I'm squiggly and wiggly. I'm furry and brown.
I spend mi days just crawling around.
I munch on leaves an' I wink at lasses.
I blow kisses, whenever one passes.

But mi rovin' days, they'll be over soon.
As I'm goin' inside mi little cocoon.
In there I'll stay for a day or two.
As a beautiful butterfly, I'll break through.

I'll stand up proud and show the world mi colours.
Mi mum says mi wings will be like no others.
Turquoise, scarlet and aquamarine,
the finest that the town has ever seen.

Now, being a vegetarian, I'll have now't from't farm.
Unless it's placed inside a barm.
You call 'em bread rolls, baps or cobs.
I'm just happy if there's one in mi gob.

The basic diet of a butterfly
is a small glass o' stout an' a homemade pie.
We're simple folk and so is our food,
you can keep your sushi. I'm not being rude.

Lowry never painted us, I'm sad to say,
his colours were black, brown and cold, slate-grey.
He painted folk wit' legs stick thin.
Bent o'er miserable an' looking grim.

I heard this rumour the other day,
that us butterflies only last for a day.
I'll tell you a secret, told by mi Uncle Trevor,
us butterflies are magical an' we live forever.

# I Wish I Were a Sandwich

I wish I were a sandwich.
Or perhaps a bacon bap.
Or a posh little cucumber one,
eaten by a very posh chap.

I wish I were a sandwich.
Maybe wholemeal or granary.
Every day I'd adjust my crust
and call myself Valerie.

I wish I were a sandwich.
Perchance, a French baguette.
I'd change my name from Valerie
to Marianne or Claudette.

I don't want to be a sandwich.
It wouldn't be much fun.
In fact, I'm rather happy
just being a hot cross bun.

## If I Were Invisible

If I were invisible
I'd have so much fun.
My bossy headteacher,
I'd kick them up the bum!

13

# A Long Poem About Shorts

Red shorts are my bed shorts,
in which I dream the night away.
Blue shorts are my new shorts,
I proudly wore them yesterday.

Yellow shorts are my mellow shorts,
in which I sit an' learn to chill.
Grey shorts are my "not okay" shorts,
which I wear when I'm feeling ill.

Black shorts are my slack shorts,
I struggle to keep them up.
Green shorts are my cuisine shorts,
in which I like to stand and cook.

Brown shorts are my down shorts,
in which I like to loaf around.
Mucky shorts are my lucky shorts,
in the pocket I found a pound.

Scarlet shorts are my market shorts,
in which I browse and like to shop.
Gold shorts are my very bold shorts,
in which I dance until I drop.

Pink shorts are my think shorts,
in which I sit and ponder all day.
Lemon shorts are my Devon shorts,
which I wear on my holiday.

Magenta shorts are my inventor shorts,
In which I like to manufacture.
Tartan shorts are my fartin' shorts,
in which I trump just like a tractor.

My orange shorts and my purple shorts,
I like to wear them all the time.
But these dudes, I seldom include,
as the words are hard to rhyme.

# Everything is Turning Blue

I'm in so much trouble but what can I do?
Everything I touch is turning to blue.

Blue is a colour that I love very much,
but not with every single thing I touch.

I'm Alex McKinley and I'm in a stew.
When I look or touch, things turn blue.

It suddenly started about a year ago.
My granny went clammy and turned **indigo**.

I must have caught it as my hands are on fire.
My clothes are bright blue, my shoes
**sapphire**.

For my dinner I had:
sausages, gravy and stew.
I pushed in my fork, it went
**navy blue**.

Miss Rosie Cooper popped
round for some sugar.
Then screamed and went **teal**, when
I tried to hug her.

Mum says she loves me, as my eyes they
twinkle.
When tucking me in she turned
**periwinkle**.

My sister hates me, if she sees me
she screams.
I kissed her on Tuesday, now she's as
blue as her jeans!

Sir asked me a question but I was
unsure.
He gave me detention so I turned him
**azure**.

My hamster Hettie has vacated the scene.
I poked her and stroked her, now she's
**aquamarine**.

Poor Terry McGinty, my old pet tortoise...
He's not well in his shell. He looks funny in
**turquoise**.

I'm totally heartbroken, I want it to stop.
When I turn people blue, they get in a strop.

I went to my doctor. He's such a nice
fellow.
He looked in my mouth, and then he
turned yellow!

"ARGH!"

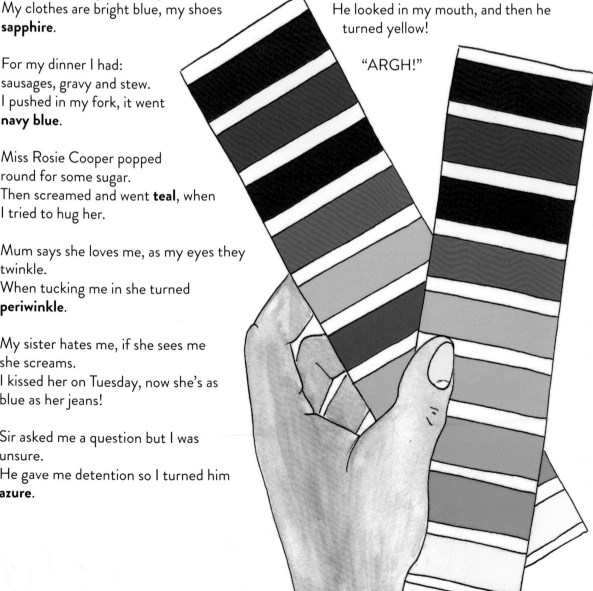

## If Mushrooms Could Talk

If mushrooms could talk,
what would they say?
What about their accent,
the words they convey?
Would they be posh
and 'well-to-do'?
Would they be common
and talk about poo?
They live in the dark
and ne'er see the sky.
But they're happy souls.
Real fungi!

# The Trumping Seagull

I fly around in all sorts of weather.
When I trump, I blow out feathers.
Surely, it must be illegal,
to be the only flying, farting seagull?

# Shut Your Cake Hole

*The setting: Inside a busy town bakery, late Saturday afternoon and the shop has just closed. The cakes begin a heated discussion:*

Narrator:      She swept the floor and cleared the clutter, and at half past six she pulled down the shutter. Yes, the bakery came alive, once the people had gone. First to speak was Sonia the Scone.

Sonia:         (Haughtily) As the spokesperson of this here shop, there are some things I'll have to stop! I remember a time when I were a lass, (waving her hand towards the glass cabinet) there were only cakes behind that glass, now we have got all these spicy things...

Jock:          (Interrupting in a Scottish accent) Excuse me, I differ to beg. We're called savouries or a Scottish Egg. Aye, Sonia, the bakery has become a more diverse place.

Lorraine:      (Nodding her head, speaking in a Brummie accent)
               I agree. Take that, Sonia. "In your face!"

Sonia:         (Angrily) Oh, shut up! You flans are all the same.

Lorraine:      I'm not a flan. I'm a quiche and my name's Lorraine.

Jock:          Sonia, that's enough, for heaven's sake. You're a scone, my dear. You're not even a cake.

Sonia:         (Lips quivering) Yes, I am, I have jam and cream. Saying I'm not a cake is totally obscene. I'll have you know that I'm famous in Devon, I am, you know, aren't I, Kevin?

Kevin:         (Rather reluctantly in a Cockney accent) Leave it be, Sonia, not that old chestnut. I'm keeping out of it; I'm just a doughnut.

Lorraine:      (Almost sobbing) Sonia, we're all sick of your horrible jibes, your cutting remarks and your negative vibes. I've got to say you're just plain nasty. You're horrible to me and Patricia the Pasty.

Jock:          Lorraine is right. Learn a lesson. Just be quiet and reel your neck in. Listen to reason. Just be told. Sonia, my love – shut your cake hole!

## Pyjama Day

My mate Billy is really bananas.
He went to school wearing pyjamas.
The headmistress got all high and mighty.
As she'd rocked up wearing her nightie.

# I'm
## a
## Pholcidae

All right, my lover, I'd like to say,
that I am indeed a Pholcidae.
Foll-sid-ay. Go on, give it a try.
Come on! Don't be shy.

I'm not a Cellar spider, that's a fact.
Nor a Golden Orb or anything like that.
Call me Daddy Long Legs if it makes you happy,
but don't be offended if I get snappy.

When I bend over, I pull funny faces.
I don't wear shoes, as I can't tie laces.
Shorter legs are what I really, really want...
but then again, I'd look like an ant.

We and giraffes have a lot in common,
our ankles are miles away from our bottoms.
When God made us, he must have been havin' a giggle.
Long lanky legs an' a little body in the middle.

It's a fact that one of my wildest dreams
is to wear leggings, trousers or jeans.
When I buy underwear, I hear their sniggers
when I ask for black eight-legged frilly knickers.

So, a Daddy Long Legs is just what I am.
The best of it is, I'm not even a man.
I close my eyes and at night I pray
that one day I'll be called a Pholcidae.

21

## Lettuce Fall in Love

Poor Barry the snail
had been unlucky in love.
'Twas only last week
that he'd been dumped by a slug.

But things were improving,
this he could tell.
She came in the form
of the lovely Michelle.

He first spotted Shelley,
munching on vegetables.
She tipped her head shyly
and fluttered her tentacles.

The sheen of her shell
was bedazzling and twirly.
A real classy lady
and nothing too girly.

She whispered, "Kiss me, Barry,
let's make them all jealous."
Poor Barry went pale and
nearly choked on his lettuce.

Shell against shell,
both crawling together.
At one mile an hour
they went hell for leather.

"Barry, you're special,
my heart it goes boom!
Let us climb to the top
of the old mushroom."

As they climbed the mushroom,
they giggled and laughed.
Slowly, they crawled
for an hour and a half.

Barry gazed at Michelle,
as this was his wish.
Slowly closing their eyes
in the moonlight they kissed.

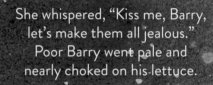

# Do Pens Go to Heaven?

Do pens go to heaven when they run out of ink?
What about thoughts when they no longer think?
What about dreams after they've been dreamt?
Sometimes a dream is heaven sent.

Do batteries go to heaven when they finally run out?
What about potatoes when they begin to sprout?
Are all clothes cheered on their arrival?
Or is heaven the place where they get recycled?

Do books go to heaven once they've been read?
What about food and mouldy old bread?
What about trains, planes and worn-out shoes?
Once in heaven, are they all brand new?

Do mosquitoes go to heaven along with midges?
What about toasters and battered old fridges?
What about an itch after it's been scratched?
Or really hard questions after they've been asked?

Do fireworks go to heaven with a mighty boom?
What about dust pans or worn-out brooms?
What about light bulbs when they no longer shine?
Or do they guide you to heaven, in a great big line?

# The Sleep Thief

Oh, blinking heck, that's all I need.
Someone's gone and stole my sleep.
I was comfortable there, in Slumber Land.
Now, in my brain, there's a marching band.

My tranquil sleep has been stolen.
In my mind, my tabs all open.
I battle alone, a thousand fears.
Whilst I ponder, do ants have ears?

A million questions I have to answer.
Is my granny really a gangster?
Do spiders speak backwards or is that a myth?
What about worms, do they have lips?

Why is silver cheaper than gold?
Do penguins ever feel the cold?
Do trees blush when they lose their leaves?
Is the moon really made of cheese?

Why is Dyslexia so hard to say?
Why not omelette, instead of Pancake Day?
Why do bugs have bottoms that glow?
When you scratch an itch, where does it go?

The egg and the chicken, who came first?
Could a pufferfish ever burst?
If dust spoke French how funny that'd be.
"Je suis poussière, bonjour mon ami."

Do clouds have feelings, the rain their tears?
Do squirrels on the Wirral ever go for a beer?
When dogs bark, do they know each other?
Why is buff the name of a colour?

These are the questions that keep me awake.
Please let me sleep, for heaven's sake.
Be gone, Sleep Thief, you are so boring.
Oh, flipping heck, now it's morning.

# Paper Twins

There were two twins,
named Evie and Layla.
Funny thing was,
they were made of paper.

They'd float to school
on the morning breeze.
But on windy days,
they get stuck in trees.

They hated walking home
on days that were foggy.
Getting home late,
all damp and soggy.

They'd wrap up warm
with a cuddle from mum.
They were scared of fire,
as it burnt their bums.

Being made of paper
really had its uses.
If you forgot your books,
there were no excuses.

Having no books
didn't cause much harm.
Layla would write stuff,
all day, on her arms.

Although they were paper,
they had looks and brains.
They were bonded in love
with invisible chains.

# The Fifth Earl of Mothsay

*(To be recited in a Scottish accent)*

I'm Lord Hughie McEwan,
the Fifth Earl of Mothsay.
They say I'm dull and boring,
but that's just hearsay.

I like to keep myself fit,
I go on long rambles.
I'm attracted to torches,
night lights and candles.

Butterflies' colours
are mentioned a lot.
But my wings are grey,
like a pepper pot.

I'm a Peppered Moth
but I won't make you sneeze.
I feed on the lichens,
which I find on trees.

On people's old clothes,
I nibble and feast.
When I see an old jumper,
I'm a dribbling beast.

Well, that's me,
my name is Lord Hugh.
Don't bother me
and I won't bother you.

I keep myself to myself.
I don't get into battles.
I'm attracted to torches,
night lights and candles.

## Mixed Up Months

September's not **November**,
nor is it **June**.
**December**'s getting excited,
Christmas is coming soon.
**Jan** and **Feb** go out for a **March**,
into the **April** rain.
**July** and **August** are far too hot
and constantly complain.
**October**'s feeling lonely
and gives **July** a call.
"I'm feeling down,
my leaves are brown,
I'm waiting for the fall."
**May** stands up to count us all,
to ensure that we're all here.
"Twelve apostles altogether
and that's another year!"

## Morning, Sir!

Bell goes, children rush.
Through the door, shove and push.
"Forgot my scarf!"
"Forgot my hat!"
Tittle tattle – chit chat.

Registration! Eyes down.
Listen to Sir, not a sound.
"Mary Burns, Tony Bell,"
Broken pencil – bombshell!

# Ig's Ig Glue

The Inuit have glue made by Ig.
It makes their homes really big.
There's only one product they will use.
A large litre tub of Ig's Ig glue.

ig's place

## It Must Be Ace to Live in Space

Floating around the Milky Way,
not knowing if it's night or day.
Saying loud, "It's high up here."
Floating above the Earth's atmosphere.

It must be ace to live in space.

Encountering aliens
of every colour and hue.
Shaking their tentacles,
saying, "How do you do?"

It must be ace to live in space.

Galactic groups gather together:
Xarjons, Rygons, Foofons and Clingers.
Counting planets and comets
on all seven fingers.

It must be ace to live in space.

Playing dot to dot,
on the planets afar.
Knowing the difference between
Venus, Saturn and Mars.

It must be ace to live in space.

# God's Been Busy

The rain, with gusto, began to pour.
Milly skipped through the kitchen door.
She jumped, sang and began to dance.
"It's okay, Mum,
it's only God watering his plants."

The thunder rumbled, the sky went black.
Mum screamed again as the lightning cracked.
"Come inside, the storm is looming."
"It's okay, Mum,
it's only God furniture moving."

With crashes and flashes the sky shone bright.
Boom! A brilliant flash of light.
Milly smiled at the sky, without a flicker.
"It's okay, Mum,
it's only God taking my picture."

# The Chicken Rap
*(To be recited in a New York rapper's accent)*

Buck-buck-buck.
Flap-flap-flap.
Shake your booty.
Scratch-scratch-scratch.
Strut your stuff, you know where it's at.
Now you're doing the Chicken Rap.
Let's all do the Chicken Rap.

Yo to ma bros, tell me what's clickin'.
I'm strutting my stuff. I hope y'all listenin'.
Down on the farm, I feel safe.
This old yard is my own safe place.

My momma's called Vic.
My poppa's called Ken.
My name's Heather, I'm a free-range hen.

**"Her name is Heather, she's a free-range hen."**

Old Pete's Farm is where I do my thing,
hatched with love, in the early spring.
When I was born, I shook my tail feather.
My momma says, "Yes! We'll call her
Heather."

I'm free range, not cooped in a pen.
My name's Heather, I'm a free-range hen.

**"Her name is Heather, she's a free-range
hen."**

Buck-buck-buck.
Flap-flap-flap.
Shake your booty.
Scratch-scratch-scratch.
Strut your stuff, you know
where it's at.
Now you're doing the Chicken Rap.
Let's all do the Chicken Rap.

My worry began when I fell from the egg.
Tiny little beak and scrawny legs.
My wings don't work, how absurd...
Who has ever heard of a flightless bird?

I lay perfect eggs, again and again.
My name's Heather, I'm a free-range hen.

**"Her name is Heather, she's a free-range hen."**

Momma says I'm her favourite daughter,
I'm halfway up the pecking order.
I'm so lucky, my life I love it.
I don't wanna be no chicken nugget.

I've got a cool sister, her name, it's Gwen.
My name's Heather, I'm a free-range hen.

**"Her name is Heather, she's a free-range hen."**

Buck-buck-buck.
Flap-flap-flap.
Shake your booty.
Scratch-scratch-scratch.
Strut your stuff, you know where it's at.
Now you're doing the Chicken Rap.
Let's all do the Chicken Rap.